Josie and the Junk Box

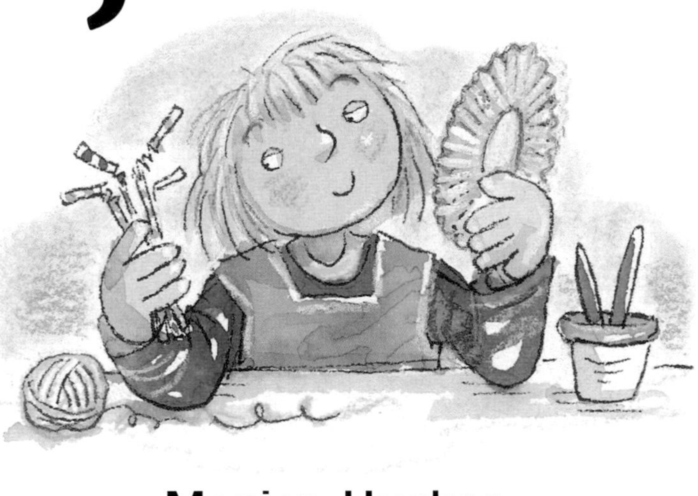

Monica Hughes
Illustrated by Lisa Smith

RIGBY

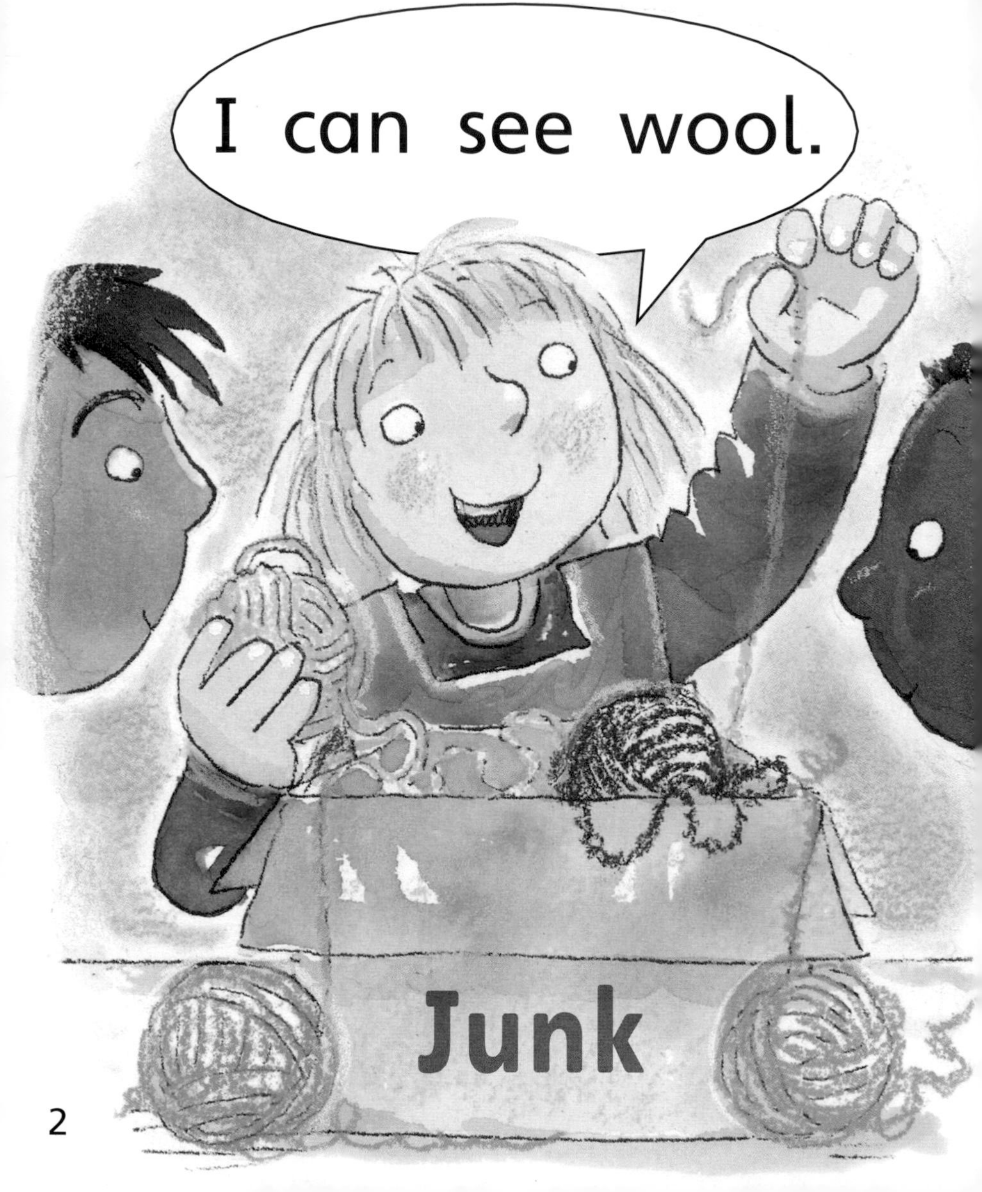
I can see wool.
Junk

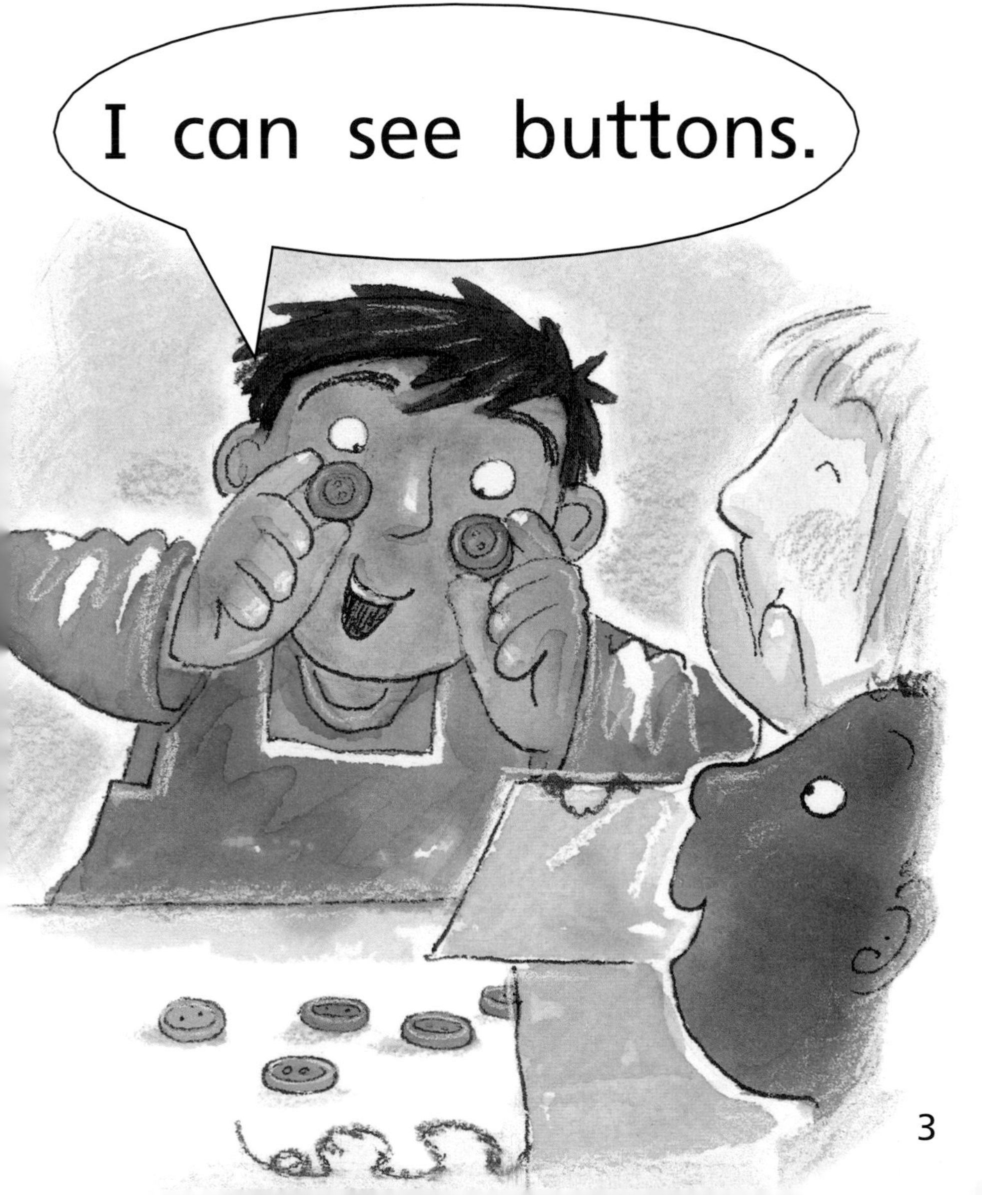
I can see buttons.

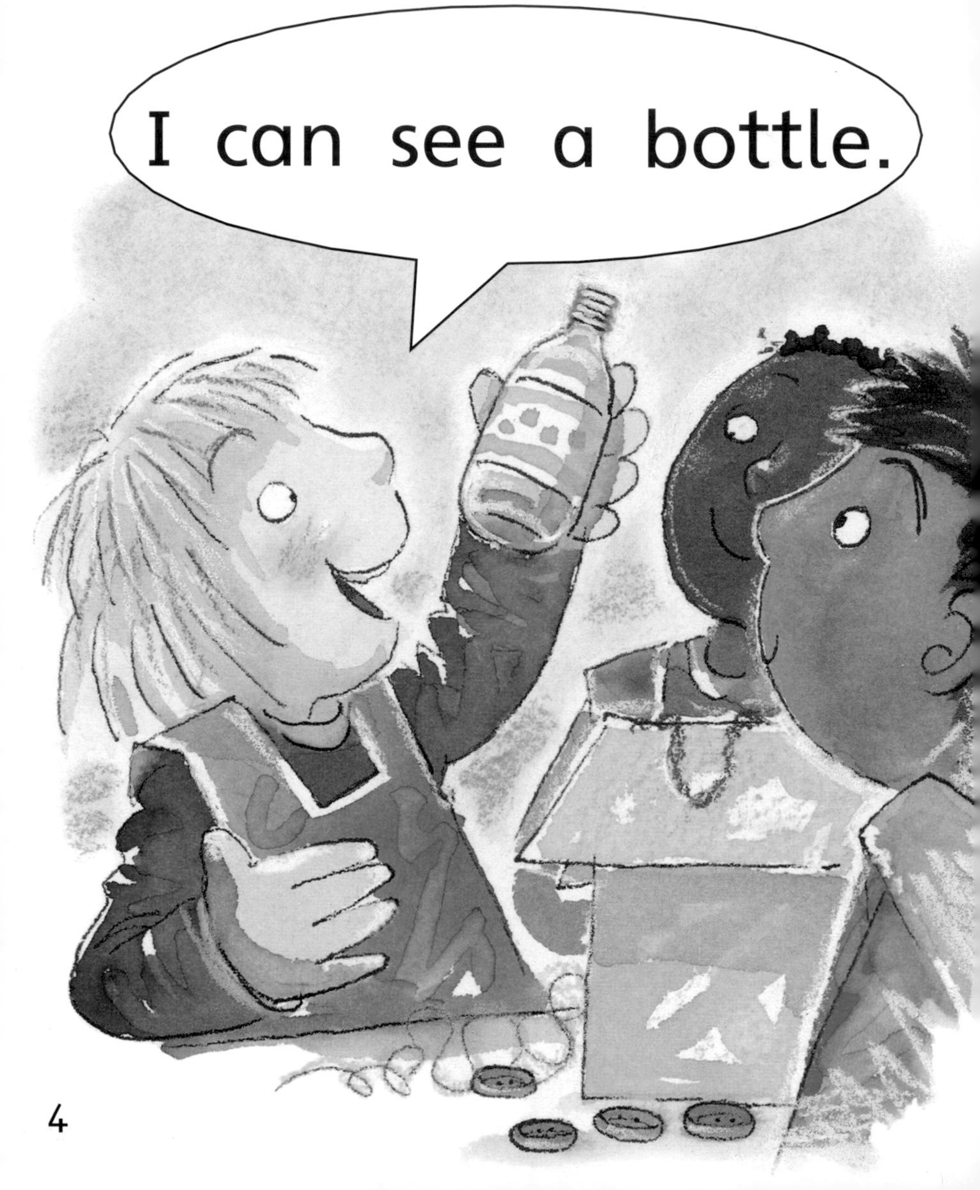
I can see a bottle.

I can see straws.

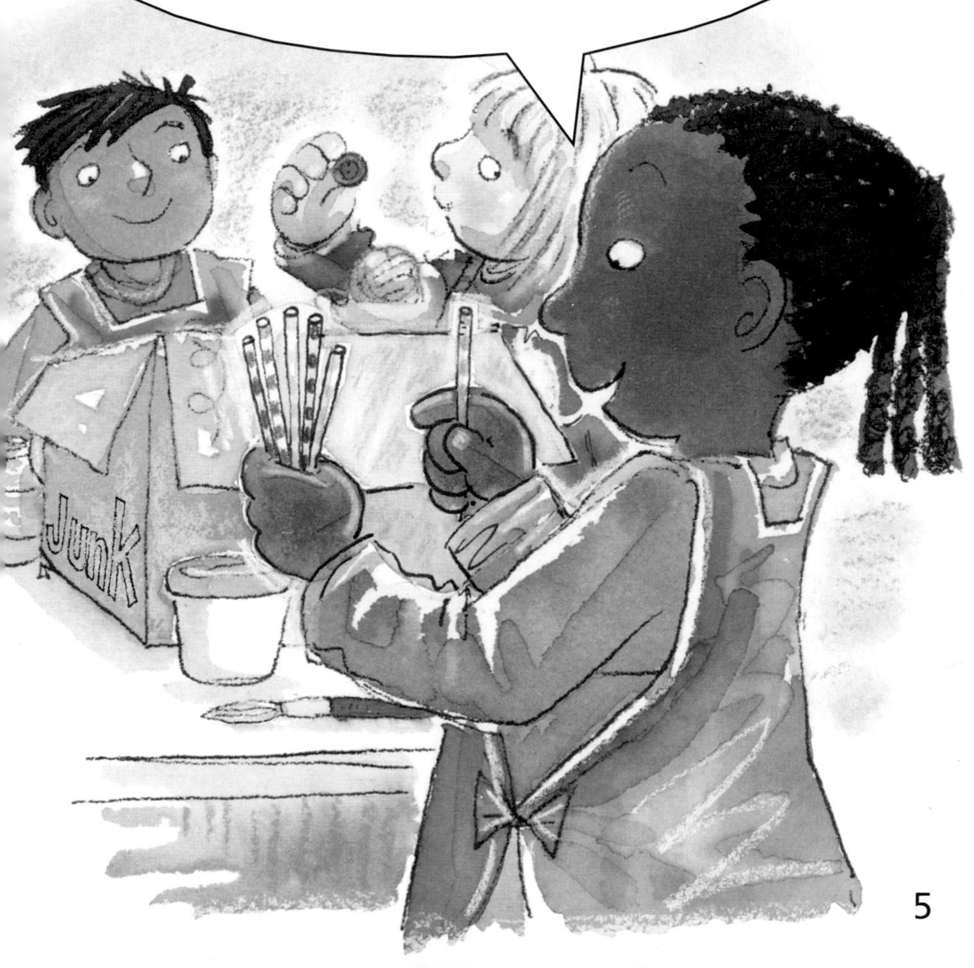

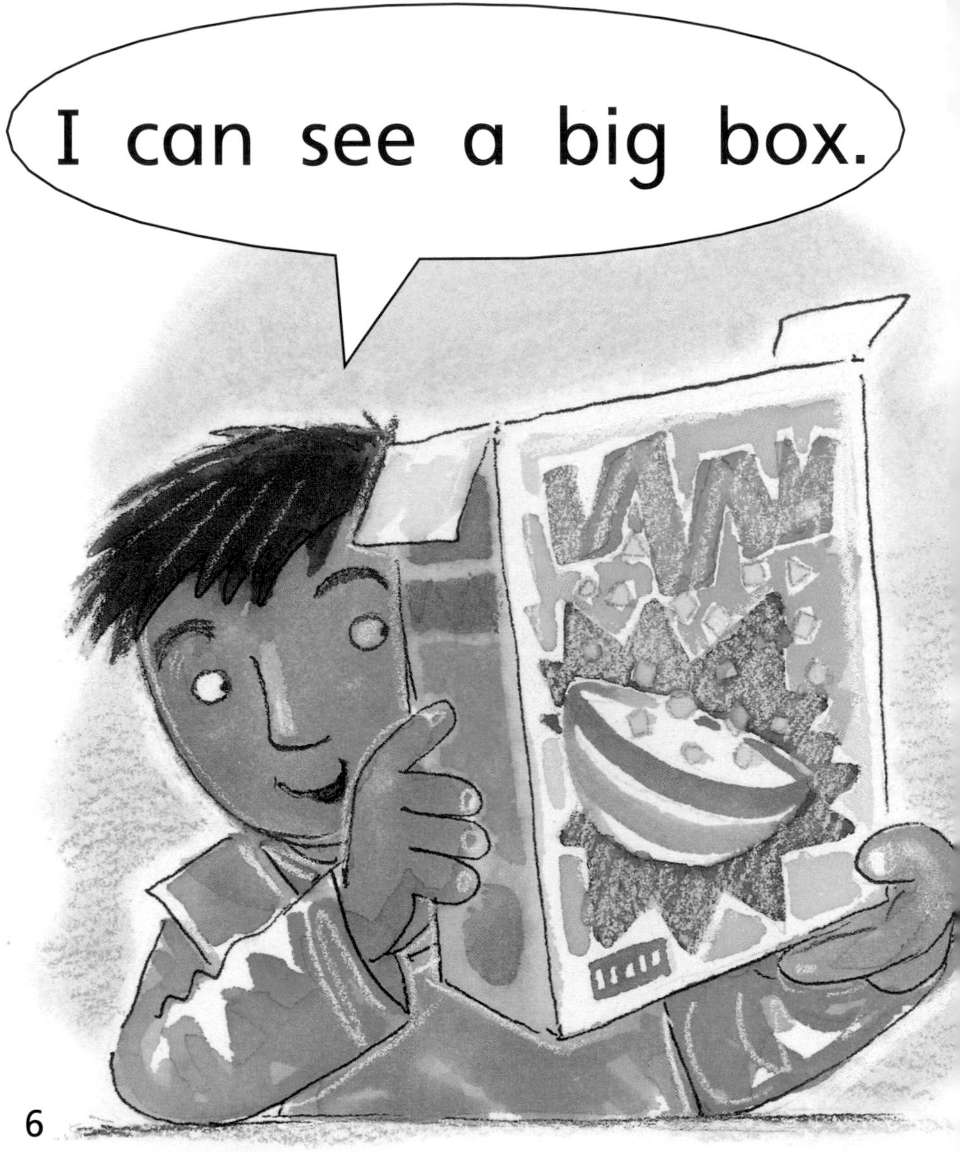
I can see a big box.

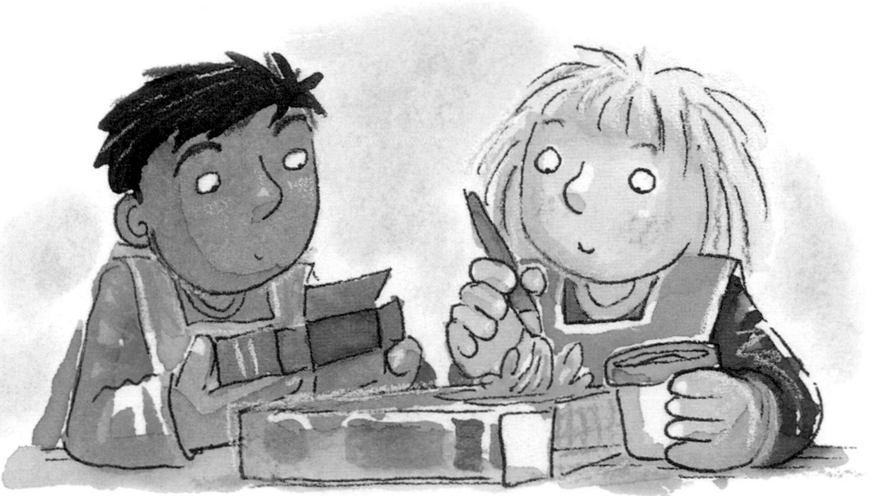

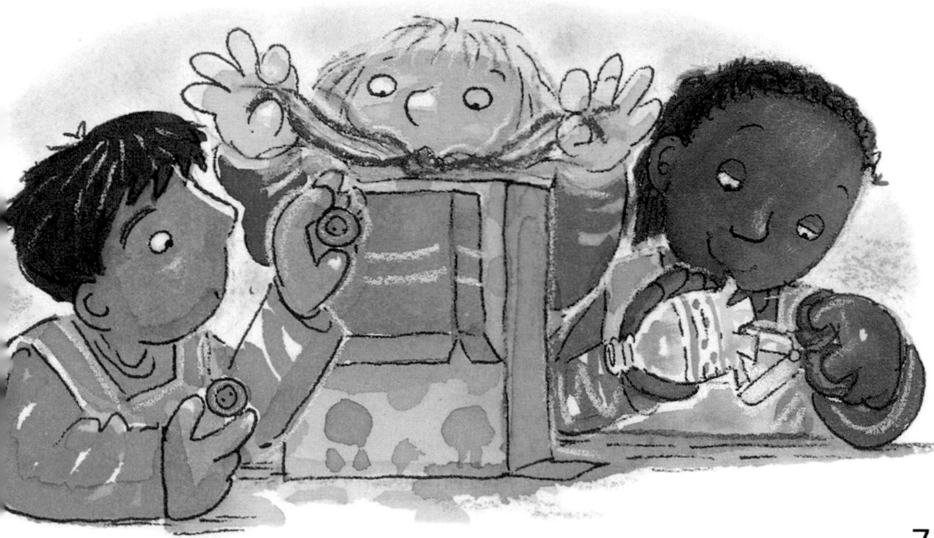

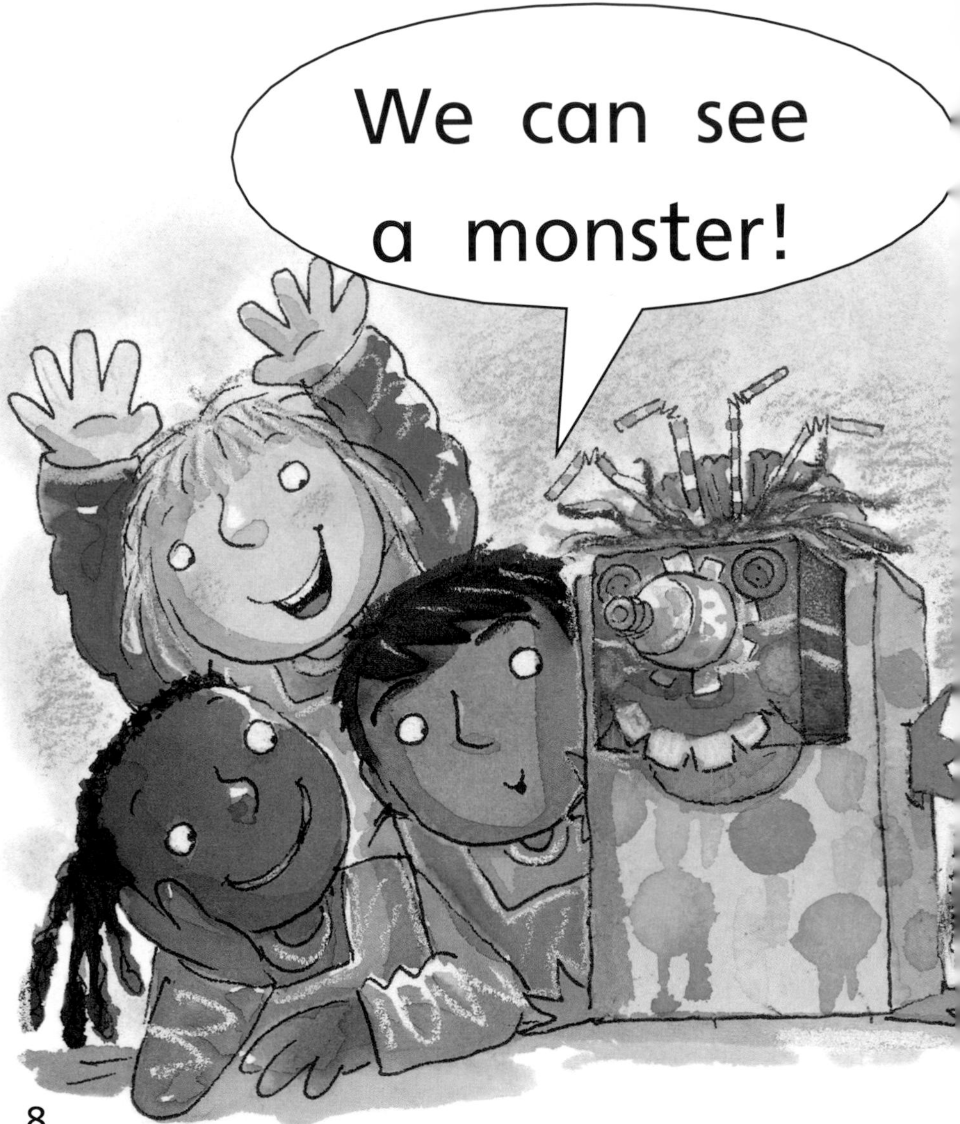
We can see a monster!